Eric Carle

The Rabbit
and the Turtle

Aesop's fables

For Nadja and Teresa

The stories in this newly released collection of Aesop's fables were originally published by Orchard Books in *Eric Carle's Treasury of Classic Stories for Children.* As both a storyteller and an illustrator, Eric Carle has achieved a compelling unity of effect that captures the homely wisdom, fantasy, and humor of these childhood favorites.

ISBN: 978-0-545-14866-5

Portions of this book appeared in *Twelve Tales from Aesop*, retold and illustrated by Eric Carle, published in 1980 by Philomel Books, New York, New York. Grateful acknowledgment is given for permission to use these materials in the current volume. Special contents of this volume copyright © 1988 by Eric Carle, Inc. Text and illustrations copyright © 1976, 1978, 1980, and 1988 by Eric Carle. All rights reserved. Published by Orchard Books, an imprint of Scholastic Inc. ORCHARD BOOKS and design are registered trademarks of Watts Publishing Group, Ltd., used under license. SCHOLASTIC and associated logos are trademarks and/or registered trademarks of Scholastic Inc.

12 11 10 9 8 7 6 5 4 3 2 1   10 11 12 13 14 15/0

Printed in the U.S.A.   08

First Scholastic paperback printing, February 2010

The Rabbit and the Turtle

Aesop's fables

retold and illustrated by Eric Carle

SCHOLASTIC INC. New York Toronto London Auckland Sydney Mexico City New Delhi Hong Kong

Contents

The Lion and the Mouse

A huge lion sitting on the grass happened to put his foot on a tiny mouse.

"Help, help!" cried the mouse. "Let me out from under here!" And she tickled the lion's paw.

The lion lifted his foot, saw the tiny mouse, and held her up to his face.

"Grrrr," growled the lion.

"Please, Mr. Lion," begged the mouse, "don't eat me."

"Why shouldn't I?" asked the lion. "I am hungry."

"I am so little," said the mouse, "I wouldn't make much of a meal for you."

"You are right," said the lion and he put the mouse down on the ground.

"Thank you," said the mouse as she scurried away. "I'll be glad to help *you* someday."

"*You* help *me?*" roared the lion, laughing. "That is a joke."

Then the lion stretched out in the shade of a tree and fell asleep. But, just as he began to snore, three wolves sneaked up and threw a heavy rope around him. Before the lion had opened his eyes he was tied securely to the tree. The wolves stole what they could carry of the lion's belongings and ran away, leaving the lion still tied to the tree. No matter how hard the lion pulled, he could not get the rope off. He could not even loosen it.

"Help, help!" howled the lion. When the mouse heard his cry she ran to him.

"Don't worry, Mr. Lion," said the mouse, "I'll help you." And with her sharp teeth she bit through the heavy ropes. In no time she had set the lion free.

"Thank you so much," said the lion, and he set out after the wolves. When he caught up with them, he threw them to the ground and took back all they had stolen from him.

"And now, my dear friend," said the lion as he returned to the mouse, "you have saved my life and my fortune, too. I see that you were not at all too small to do very big deeds!"

"My pleasure," replied the mouse proudly.

Friends come in all sizes and shapes.

The Wolf and the Dog

A poorly dressed wolf with an empty stomach happened to meet a well-fed and well-dressed dog.

"Ah, hello, Cousin," said the wolf. "How are you?"

"Don't call me 'Cousin,'" answered the dog. "Look at you! In tatters. And begging. It's disgusting! Disgraceful!"

"What a beautiful dress you are wearing," the wolf went on, "and you have such nice plump cheeks. It's clear that you don't know what it is to be hungry."

"I work for my master and he takes good care of me," answered the dog.

"I would like to work for your master, too," said the wolf, "if he'd take as much care of me."

"Well, it just so happens," said the dog, "that my master does need more help."

"What kind of help?"

"We need another watchdog."

"Can I do that?"

"Surely, it's easy. Come along."

As they walked toward the master's house the wolf noticed something around the dog's neck.

"Cousin, what is that thing around your neck?"

"That is a collar."

"What is a collar for?"

"One can attach a chain to it."

"A chain? Whatever for?"

"Watchdogs are often tied on chains outside their masters' houses. Didn't you know that?"

"Thank you, Cousin," said the wolf, turning around. "I know that I'd rather be hungry than chained up like a slave."

And with that the wolf said goodbye and left.

Being free is the greatest gift.

The Fox and the Crane

A stingy fox once invited a crane to his house for dinner. He served a delicious meal but he put it on very flat plates. The poor crane, with her long beak, could not get at the food at all. She turned her neck this way and that way but it didn't help. The food always slipped away from her beak. The fox, pretending not to see the crane's trouble, gobbled up all the food in no time. Of course, the crane was still hungry after the table had been cleared.

"Dear Miss Crane," said the fox as the crane was leaving, "I hope that you have enjoyed your meal. Let's get together soon again."

The crane nodded her head politely, but she did not reply. However, soon afterward, the crane invited the fox to her house for dinner. She, too, served a delicious meal—but in very tall, thin goblets. Of course the fox couldn't get at the food! He tried this way and he tried that way but it didn't help. His food was down at the bottom of the goblet, and no matter how he tried, he couldn't reach it. In the meantime the crane put her long beak down into her tall, thin goblet and easily ate up her meal. This time it was the fox who was still hungry after the table had been cleared.

"Dear Mr. Fox," said the crane as the fox was leaving, "I hope that you have enjoyed your meal. Let's get together soon again."

But the embarrassed fox never again called on the crane.

Treat others as you want to be treated.

The Cat and the Mouse

A young mouse, sick and tired of being chased by the cat, had an idea. The mouse called in the whole family and proclaimed, "We mice must protect ourselves from the cat, once and for all!"

"Yes, yes!" cried all the mice.

"We must be able to run around freely any time and anywhere we wish to do so."

"Right, right!" shrieked the other mice.

"I know how to outwit the cat," the proud young mouse went on.

"How?" asked the others.

"With this bell," said the young mouse, pointing to a shiny new bell. "When the cat is asleep we shall fasten the bell around his neck. When he moves, the bell will ring. That way we can hear the cat before the cat sneaks up on us."

"Bravo, bravo!" cried the mice.

The young mouse bowed and smiled.

"Long live our genius!" shouted the mice.

The young mouse took another bow.

"Question," said a weak voice from the back of the room. "Who will put the bell around the cat's neck?"

All the mice turned around to look at their grandmother, who had asked the question. She was an old mouse, wrinkled and stooped.

"A volunteer, of course," answered the young mouse.

"Who will volunteer?" asked the grandmother.

Everybody looked at everybody else. No one volunteered. And that is why cats still catch mice, to this very day.

An idea is not always enough.

The Monkey and the Fox

When the wise and beloved old king of the jungle died, all the animals got together to elect a new ruler. Each animal told the others why he would be the best king. When it was the monkey's turn, he put on the old king's crown and his velvet robe and did a wonderful imitation of the king. He even made a short speech in the old king's voice.

"It's almost like having our dear king back again," said the animals and they promptly elected the monkey to be their new king. Only the fox disagreed. He tried to warn the other animals that they were making a mistake.

"It is not enough to be able to imitate the old king," said the fox. "The monkey is good at that, but he has no sense at all. He certainly is not wise enough to be your leader."

But the animals did not listen to him.

A few days later the fox noticed a trap in the forest. The people from the zoo had put it up to catch the monkey.

"I have noticed something curious in the jungle," said the fox to the monkey.

"Let's go and look at it," answered the monkey.

Soon they came to a large net with a banana hanging under the middle of it. Without thinking twice, the monkey reached for the banana. As he touched the fruit the net fell over him. The monkey was caught. The people who had hidden behind the trees rushed out, tied up the monkey and took him to their zoo. A little later the fox went to the zoo and visited the monkey.

"You traitor," cried the monkey. "You have betrayed your king."

"You have betrayed yourself," said the fox. "A king who falls for the first trap that has been set for him is not a good king. A king who is so foolish would not serve his animals well."

And that is the truth.

Do not try to be something you are not.

The Wolf and the Lamb

A wolf met a lamb and said to her, "I am hungry. I am going to eat you up."

"My dear wolf," said the lamb, "I understand that perfectly well. That's the way things go. I shall not complain."

"You are a good girl," said the wolf and opened his mouth, showing all his sharp teeth.

"One moment, sir," said the lamb. "As you know, I am entitled to have one last wish."

"That is so, my dear," said the wolf, "and what shall that be?"

"If you would be so kind, I'd like you to play me some music," said the lamb. "I adore music."

The wolf pulled a flute from his pocket and began playing the most beautiful music he could, inspired by the thought of the delectable meal he was about to enjoy.

"You are an artist," whispered the lamb. "Do keep on playing."

Soon the shepherd, hearing unfamiliar music among his lambs, looked to see what was the matter. When he saw the murderous wolf, the shepherd took a big stick and hit the wolf over the head.

"Ouch!" yelped the wolf, and he ran into the woods.

When faced with danger, make wise choices.

The Frog and the Ox

Mr. Frog took his family for a stroll. And Mr. Ox took *his* family for a stroll.

As the two families were passing each other, one of the frog children said, "My, look how BIG that ox is!"

"I could be as big as that ox if I wanted to," said Mr. Frog and puffed himself up a little.

"There's no need to puff yourself up like that," said Mrs. Frog, "I like you just the way you are."

"I'm going to be as big as that ox," said Mr. Frog and he puffed himself up some more.

"Papa," said the other frog child, "you were just the right size before."

But Mr. Frog puffed himself up even more, his face turning red.

"Baaaa!" screamed the frog baby, alarmed by the way he looked.

But Mr. Frog puffed himself up still more, his face turning purple.

"Please!" shouted the whole frog family. "Don't! We love you the way you are."

But the frog puffed himself up even more than that. The buttons on his coat popped, his pants ripped, and his shirt split.

"Stop!" cried Mrs. Frog.

But Mr. Frog gave one more puff and EXPLODED into a thousand pieces.

"Did you hear something go *pop?*" Mr. Ox asked his wife.

"No," replied Mrs. Ox as they walked on.

Be proud of who you are.

The Blackbird and the Peacocks

One day a young blackbird saw some peacocks. From that moment on, his life was changed.

"Oh, how beautiful they are," he whispered to himself, "and how ugly I am."

Day and night he thought of their beauty. He could neither sleep nor eat.

"If only I could be one of them," moaned the poor blackbird.

He began to follow the peacocks around and when any of them dropped one of its gorgeous feathers, the blackbird would rush to pick it up. Soon he had many of the lovely feathers. He stuck them into his belt.

"Now I am one of them," said the young blackbird as he gazed at his reflection in the mirror. And he flew out to join the peacocks.

He strutted in front of them proudly. But the peacocks had never seen anything so silly as a blackbird with peacock feathers stuck in his belt.

"Ha-ha-ha-ha . . . " they laughed, holding their sides.

A bunch of blackbirds, attracted by all the noise, came out to see what was going on. They, too, had never seen anything so silly as a blackbird dressed up in peacock feathers.

"Ha-ha-ha-ha . . . " they laughed, holding their sides.

The young blackbird ignored them all. "I am a peacock," he insisted.

"The poor creature is touched in the head," said the peacocks.

"Those fine feathers won't fool anyone," agreed the blackbirds. "He is still a blackbird underneath."

Do not pretend to be someone you are not.

The Fox and the Crow

A crow sat high up in a tree with some food in his beak. Below on a park bench sat Mrs. Fox with her son.

"Mama," said the little fox, looking up at the bird, "I wish I had something to eat."

"You *will*," whispered Mrs. Fox into his ear. "Just watch this."

Then, in a slightly louder voice, for the crow to hear, she went on.

"Oh that crow is *so* handsome!"

Upon hearing this, the crow ruffled his feathers. He was very pleased.

"Look at his beautiful, shiny coat!"

The crow felt so proud.

"And see his elegant manners!"

If the crow had been a cat he would have purred, that's how happy he felt to hear all these nice things.

"It is said that the crow has a wonderful voice."

"I shall show them how well I can sing," thought the bird, and he opened his beak to do so.

At that, the food he had been holding fell down to the ground next to the foxes.

"Here, son," said Mrs. Fox and handed him the crow's lunch. "Didn't I tell you that you'd have something good to eat?"

And the crow began to sing.

"Come, son," said Mrs. Fox. "Let's move away from here. I find the crow's song so very irritating."

Common sense is greater than beauty.

The Grasshopper and the Ants

All summer long the grasshopper played his fiddle and sang songs. It was a pleasant way to live. Everyone enjoyed his music and he had many friends. There was plenty of food, free for the taking, in the green summer fields. The grasshopper just nibbled a little here and a little there, and then moved on.

The ants, on the other hand, worked hard all summer long collecting food and storing it in their houses.

When it began to get cold, and the snow fell, the grasshopper shivered. His stomach was empty so he went from ant house to ant house, begging for something to eat.

"While you fiddled last summer," said the ants, "we worked hard putting grain away for the wintertime. Now we have just enough for ourselves. Let us alone. Go away."

Poor grasshopper. He was getting hungrier and colder and was beginning to think he would starve to death. Night came and the grasshopper started sadly down the road that led away from the town where everyone had so cruelly refused him food.

Just then he passed the last house. Through the window the grasshopper saw some ants preparing for a holiday feast. Once more he knocked on the door to ask for food. This time, a friendly ant opened it and saw her summertime companion, the grasshopper. Before the grasshopper could say a word, she shouted to her family, "Look! Tonight we shall have music!" To the grasshopper she said, "Come in and play and be merry with us."

Together they all celebrated. The ants brought out their most luscious food and the grasshopper played his sweetest music. They danced and they ate and they sang all night long. And everybody was happy.

Always prepare today for tomorrow.

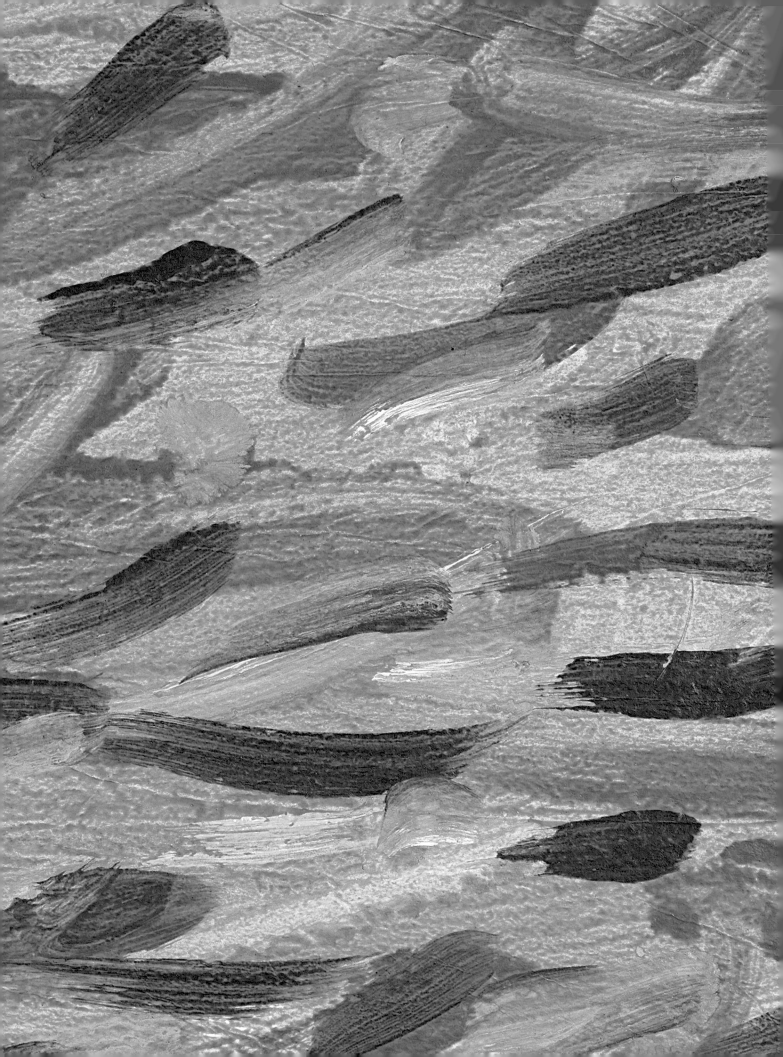